Weekly Reader Children's Book Club presents

Tales of Mr. Pengachoosa

TALES OF
MR. PENGACHOOSA

by Caroline Rush

Pictures by Dominique Michele Strandquest

Crown Publishers, Inc.
New York

Also by Caroline Rush

THE SCARECROW

Weekly Reader Children's Book Club Edition

❧ Contents ❧

Tales of Mr. Pengachoosa

❧ I ❧

The Snow House

It all started one winter after I had had rheumatic fever, and I was told that I must stay indoors during extra bad weather. Somehow that winter the weather seemed to be nearly always extra bad, and I seemed to spend so much time looking into the rainy garden, or watching the other children playing in the snow, that my father brought me home a hamster as a pet, to keep me company.

And that was really how it all began. I called him Hammy,

3

and, though he did not like being stroked, he loved to sit quietly in my cupped hands and wash himself.

One day in early December, when my sisters had gone to a Christmas party and the house was very quiet, we sat together by the fire, and I seemed to notice that among his squeaks there were some that almost sounded like words. I was amazed, and I found that when I listened very closely I could catch one or two words, and then even whole sentences.

He seemed to be talking about someone called Mr. Pengachoosa, and as I listened more and more carefully I began to undertsand that Mr. Pengachoosa was his grandfather. Hammy talked so softly and quickly that it was almost as if it came from my own head, and just as I was beginning to understand nearly every word my sisters came home. They banged the front door and started running upstairs laughing, and Hammy stopped talking altogether when they burst into the room.

I told them what had happened but they did not even try to believe me, and when they had gone out again, even though I listened very carefully I could not hear a word, so I hardly believed it myself.

One day about a week later, when we were sitting on the window seat watching the snow falling outside, very softly he began again to tell me about his grandfather, and this time

I understood. It was about Mr. Pengachoosa and the big snowstorm. . . .

Mr. Pengachoosa had been staying with friends in the country. It had been snowing for days, but, on this morning it was different, clear and sunny, and Mr. Pengachoosa decided to go for a walk.

At first it was lovely, and he had walked quite a long way from the house when it started to snow again. Great white flakes tumbled down, and Mr. Pengachoosa soon found that they had covered up his footsteps behind him, and he could not see his way back.

So round and round he wandered, getting snowier every minute, until he saw ahead of him in the snow a little house, but when he went up to ask the way he found that it was rather a strange little house, for it had no doors, just windows, and they were all open with the snow blowing in. And as he drew nearer he found it was hardly a house at all, just one little room with windows all around, but it looked dry so he climbed in.

Inside it was warm and still, which was surprising, for on the floor there were piles of snow that had blown in, and when he had grown used to the dim light he saw, hanging up in front of him on the wall, there was a sign. It said:

YOU MAY CHOOSE ANY PICTURE

At first he could not see any pictures. Then he noticed them stacked up against the walls. There were paintings of all shapes and sizes. So Mr. Pengachoosa went up to one of them to have a closer look.

It was a painting of cows in a meadow and as he looked at it he found that he could smell very faintly the scent of meadow grass and clover, and when he put his ear to it, he could hear far off the faint mooing of cows.

The next picture was of boats in a harbor, and at this one he caught the slight smell of seaweed, and heard the distant crying of gulls.

And so he went around, examining each picture, and trying to make up his mind which to choose. Until at last he came to one, a little one, standing alone, that he liked best.

It was just a picture of a little girl standing in the snow and smiling, and on her hands she had a little white muff, and on her head a soft white hat. She had such a friendly face, and seemed to be smiling so particularly for Mr. Pengachoosa that he decided to choose her. As he picked up the picture he noticed that what he had thought was snow beside the painting was really a pile of soft white feathers, and when he picked them up he found they were a muff and hood just like the ones the little girl wore in the picture, so he put them under his jacket with the painting, had one more look around, and climbed out of the window. The snow had stopped and he found his way home quickly.

It was the next day, when he set out to find the little house again, that he became surprised, for though he trotted up and down the hills and around the woods he could not find it. All the next day he searched, and the next, and all the while the snow was melting. Soon it became too slippery for walking far.

So it was not until the last day, when the snow had quite gone, that he found the little house again, and when he saw it he understood why it had no doors. For in front of him was a tall tower and right on top was his little house. When he had come first the snow had been so deep that it had almost covered the tower, and what he had thought was a little house was really the top room of the tower sticking out above the snow.

So he never did manage to get into the little picture room again, and the next day he left for . . .

My hamster stopped suddenly and ran into his nest box, for someone below had begun banging the gong loudly for tea.

"Please don't stop now," I said. "Didn't he ever manage to get back?"

"Never enough snow," said my hamster shortly. "Now run along because I need my sleep and you need your tea."

"But please, tell me first what happened to the muff and hood?"

"They melted," he said sleepily. "When the snow went."

"And the picture of the little girl?"

But his eyes were shutting.

"Don't you notice anything?" he said. "Look in the hall near the front door." And his eyes were tight shut.

And as I went down to tea I looked, and behind the door in the hall was a picture that I had never really looked at before, of a little girl with a muff and hood, standing in the snow and smiling.

❧ 2 ❧

The Mermaid

One day my father had his study redecorated, and I stood on the landing and watched some of the things carried by to be stored in the attic. One of them was a large oblong glass tank, with the back painted to look like under-the-water, and in it was a big stuffed fish.

When the workmen had gone down again, I took Hammy up to the attic to look at it. I carried him in my hand and let him run around on the top of the case.

10

"You wouldn't think that this fish was a demon," said my hamster suddenly. "But he was, in fact he was nearly the end of my poor grandfather. You see it was like this. . . ."

Mr. Pengachoosa used to like punting, and on hot summer days he would take the punt deep into the rushes on the edge of the lake, where no one could see him, and then he would lie back in the sun and sleep.

One day as he was dozing with his hat over his eyes, he felt a little wind lift it off and blow it onto the water where it floated like a large lily leaf. Mr. Pengachoosa got up and reached for the punt pole, but just as he was going to put it into the water, he saw a little white hand reach up out of the water, catch hold of his hat, and pull it under. Mr. Pengachoosa could hardly believe his eyes and stared at the few bubbles floating where his hat had been.

Then quickly he took a deep breath and dived splashily overboard to see who the little white hand had belonged to. Underneath the water it was quite dark and very quiet, and in front of him, Mr. Pengachoosa saw a mermaid trying on his hat. She was looking up, and when he looked up too he saw that the surface of the water was silver like a looking glass, and she was admiring her reflection, and smiling when the hat fell over her face, as it kept doing as it was too big.

11

She was only a little mermaid and not very old. In her hair she wore a water lily, while around her neck (to Mr. Pengachoosa's surprise) she had twined a necklace of old black water weed.

When she saw Mr. Pengachoosa looking at her she beckoned to him to join her.

"Play with me for a while," she said. "I get so lonely. My mother and father put me in this lake as they say that the sea is too dangerous for me until I get bigger, but . . ." she paused. "They did not know it but they were wrong." And at this, tears like silver bubbles ran down her cheeks. But when Mr. Pengachoosa asked her what her father and mother did not know, and why they were wrong, she only shook her head and would not answer. But she took him by the hand and pointed.

"Look over there. Can you see the dabchick's feet?"

There they were, coming through the silver surface. Mr. Pengachoosa and the little mermaid could not see the dabchick; just his feet paddling by.

Mr. Pengachoosa found that if he filled his cheek pouches with air he could stay under for quite a long time. Together they saw many strange things; frogs and newts, and they chased water beetles, and once, in the distance, they saw hanging down from the surface, on an almost invisible thread, a hook with a worm on it.

13

But when the little mermaid thought Mr. Pengachoosa was not looking he saw tears running down her cheeks, and every now and then she gave a deep sad sigh.

There was one part of the lake where she would not let him go. It was a dark part, where the weeds were black and slimy, like the ones around her neck, and when he started in that direction she pulled at his arm and begged him to come away.

Now Mr. Pengachoosa decided to give her a surprise to cheer her up, and so, when she was not looking, he started to pick long strands of water weed, the pretty ferny sort, and began, behind his back, to braid them into a long green necklace. And at last, when they had been all around the lake and were back by his boat, and she was sitting down, he crept up behind her and broke off the strange dark necklace to put the new one in its place. No sooner had she felt the old necklace broken than she laughed out loud, and turned around smiling. But when she saw it in his hands her face dropped and she stared at him in pity. For Mr. Pengachoosa felt the necklace begin to writhe and wriggle in his hands, and then, though he tried to stop it, it wound itself as tight as a steel band around his neck and he could not get it off.

"Oh, Mr. Pengachoosa," she said. "Poor, kind Mr. Pengachoosa, you have saved me from the spell of the great fish, but you have been caught in my place." And then she gasped

14

and stared at him in horror. "He was saving me until I was fatter, but you . . ." and she looked at Mr. Pengachoosa's fat tummy, ". . . are so fat already that he will probably eat you straight away. . . . *Whoops!*"

Here my hamster stopped suddenly, for as he had been telling me his story, he had gone closer and closer to the edge of the case, and at the last word he tumbled over the edge onto the floor.

As I picked him up off the floor I asked what had happened to poor Mr. Pengachoosa, but he was cross because I had not asked whether he had hurt himself, and would not speak. He just sat on my hand like an ordinary hamster, washing the dust off his feet.

And beg as I might, he would not tell me. Until two hours later, just as I was going to bed I went to his box and pleaded.

"Did he eat him, Hammy? Did the great fish eat poor Mr. Pengachoosa?"

At that my hamster looked up and said:

"Of course not! Really you are silly, you could have guessed what happened."

"What happened?"

"Your grandfather caught him, the big fish I mean. It was your grandfather's hook and worm that Mr. Pengachoosa had seen. And as soon as the great fish was caught, the black weed necklace floated away. Anyway you have been looking at the fish all afternoon, and I am sure that if he had eaten Mr. Pengachoosa he would not have looked so happy. No one could eat someone like Mr. Pengachoosa without getting indigestion!"

❧ 3 ❧

The Wind Birds

One windy morning I was cleaning out the old toy cupboard. It had been my father's toy cupboard when he was a little boy, and as I was taking out everything, I found at the back a few things that had belonged to him.

One was a little red kite, very torn. As I put it aside to mend it, I heard a soft voice behind me.

"Funny," it said. "I thought it was bigger."

"What was bigger?" I asked, for it was Hammy, who was sitting up watching me.

17

"The kite," he said. "I would not have thought it could have carried him." Then when he saw that I was going to ask more questions, he hurried on. . . .

You see, it was a windy morning, just like today, when Mr. Pengachoosa went down to the village. He had with him his large black umbrella, and as he walked along the wind tugged and pulled at it. It pulled so hard that sometimes Mr. Pengachoosa found that his feet were off the ground, and then just as this happened, an extra big gust came and away he flew. He held very tight to the umbrella handle and hoped that he would come down soon, but the higher he went, the stronger the wind became until he was bowling along in the air.

All around him he could hear the rush of the wind. Sometimes it shrieked and whistled just like giant birds, and sometimes the beat of it sounded just like great birds' wings beating all around him, and as he sailed on the whistling and shrieking of the wind became more birdlike and the rush of the wind more than ever like wings, so that when he shut his eyes he felt that he was being carried away by a great flock of wild birds. But when he opened them he could see nothing. Then he remembered that he had heard stories about wind birds: a strange flock of wild wind birds that fly in the upper sky. You cannot see them, they said, only feel them.

Away they carried poor Mr. Pengachoosa, over the hills and lakes, far away from his home, and still he held tightly to the handle of his umbrella.

After a while he saw in the distance a tall cliff, and as they got nearer he saw that it was covered with ledges. On every ledge there was an enormous nest, and as he came nearer still he saw that the nests were all made of things that the wind blows away: lots of hats and leaves, paper and washing, all sorts of umbrellas mostly blown inside out, and kites. Just as he reached the cliff his own umbrella, with a crack, turned inside out, and he began to sink down onto one of the ledges, and he felt himself gently placed onto the edge of a nest by an invisible wind bird.

He noticed that all the things that had been blowing with him, some hats and a scarf, were blown carefully onto other nests.

Then the wind birds began to race around. Mr. Pengachoosa could see when one of them settled in a nest for all the things in it began to shake. Then he had rather a worrying thought; he was part of a nest. His nest was made up of two hats and a balloon, lots of leaves and tiles, a little red kite, and Mr. Pengachoosa.

After a while the wind birds left again to blow away more things for their nests, and when they had gone Mr. Pengachoosa sat down to think. He thought of his house and his friends, his nice warm bed, and lastly his supper, and he decided that something must be done.

He looked down to see whether he could climb down, but it was too steep. He looked up to see if he could climb up, but that was too steep as well. He could not get along the ledge, so he sat down to think again. Then he saw the kite, and when he went closer he found that it was not torn at all but quite new, so he gathered up the trailing lead, tied it carefully around him, and waited for the wind birds to come back.

At last in the distance he saw a lot of straw blowing, then some leaves and a hat, and then with a swoosh and a rush the wind birds were back. Around the cliff they roared and then started to whirl away again, but before they had gone, Mr. Pengachoosa had stood on the edge, shut his eyes tight, and then thrown the kite into the air as hard as he could.

Away went the kite and away went Mr. Pengachoosa under it. On and on they blew, and down below all the trees began to shake as they flew over them.

Back over the hills and lakes, till at last, Mr. Pengachoosa saw his own house. Then he did a very brave thing. Carefully he untied the knot around his waist; then, using all four paws, he started to slide down the string to where it trailed along the ground. Though the wind birds jerked and pulled the kite he came down so fast that he even managed to wind the end of the string around a tree trunk by running around it, panting, three times. Then, though they pulled and buffeted the kite, they could not get it, and at last swooped away, leaving the little kite, very torn now, to drift to earth, where it was gathered up and carried indoors.

Hammy suddenly stopped and looked at his pink paws. "My poor grandfather never did grow hairs on his paws again after that. In fact neither did any of us who came after. You can always tell one of his descendants as they always have bare paws. But he quite soon forgot about it, for as he was putting away the kite, he found caught in it a strange gray feather that looked more like a piece of cloud than a feather."

Then my sister came in.

"What are you doing?" she said.

"Mending this kite I found." My sister leaned forward.

"Look," she said, "Here's a feather." And she held up a gray feather. "I wonder what bird it is from."

"Maybe a wind bird's feather," I said.

"Don't be silly," said my sister. "It must be a wood pigeon's feather."

But I saw my hamster smile and wink a little, just before he disappeared into his nest box.

❧ 4 ❧

The Seasons

One day my mother gave me the job of cleaning out her workbasket. I was putting all the spools of thread neatly together and sorting out the buttons, snaps, and zippers, when among the buttons I found one that I particularly liked. It was a little yellow button shaped to look like a primrose, and though it was clearly off a little girl's dress, neither my sisters nor I had ever had buttons like that.

So I showed it to my hamster and he looked very interested.

"I always wondered where it got to," he said. And then he settled down to tell me the story. . . .

One spring Mr. Pengachoosa bought himself a bicycle, and every afternoon he would pedal around the countryside. My hamster was a baby at the time and he remembered lying in his nurse's arms watching while two strong men helped Mr. Pengachoosa onto the high seat of the bicycle.

One day as Mr. Pengachoosa was out cycling he came to a steep hill, and just as he started to pedal up he heard a small voice behind him asking for a lift up the hill. Mr. Pengachoosa turned around and there, standing on the side of the road, he saw a lovely little girl. She was wearing a green dress that looked just like soft primrose leaves, and all down the front were little yellow primrose buttons, while on her head was a crown of violets.

Mr. Pengachoosa got down and put the little girl on his seat, and began to push the bicycle uphill, and as he pushed he did strange little dances with his feet and toes to make her laugh. At first she smiled, then she giggled, and then she laughed out loud and she was still laughing when they reached the top of the hill and she got down. But before she left she pulled a button off her dress and gave it to him.

24

"Take this button," she said. "It's a magic one and when you turn it you will get a wish, but remember it will only work once, so don't turn it until you really want something." Then she smiled and skipped away, and Mr. Pengachoosa tucked it into his waistcoat pocket to save until he should really need it—and forgot all about it.

About three months later, when he was cycling around, he again found himself at the bottom of the same steep hill, and again he heard a voice asking for a lift up the hill. But this time, instead of the girl it was a boy, very brown and sunburned, with bare feet and dressed in what Mr. Pengachoosa could have sworn were green leaves neatly sewn together.

So again Mr. Pengachoosa got down, and began to push the boy on the bicycle up the hill, and as he pushed he flapped his ears until the boy began to laugh. When they reached the top the boy jumped down, but before he left he pulled from his shirt a red poppy flower and gave it to Mr. Pengachoosa.

"Keep it," he said. "It is a magic flower and will make anyone who smells it fall into a deep sleep and when he wakes up he will have forgotten everything that has happened before. But don't waste it as it only works once." Then he waved goodbye and ran off. Mr. Pengachoosa carefully tucked it away—and forgot all about it.

About three months later when he was again cycling to

the big hill, he was not surprised when he reached the bottom to hear a voice asking for a lift up. This time the asker was a little girl, dressed in red and brown and Mr. Pengachoosa noticed that her dress really was made of autumn leaves sewn together, and on her head he saw a circle of berries. He helped her onto the seat, and as they went up he kept pretending to slip and the little girl laughed merrily.

"My brother and sister have told me about you," she said when they reached the top, "and my other brother is longing to meet you. He will be here in about three months' time." Then she pulled a nut out of her pocket and gave it to him. "Keep it till you need it," she said. "The person who eats it will never feel hungry again." Then she smiled at Mr. Pengachoosa and ran off. Mr. Pengachoosa put the nut in his pocket—and forgot all about it.

About three months later Mr. Pengachoosa set off for the hill, hoping to meet the other brother. It was winter now and very cold, but sure enough as soon as he reached the bottom of the hill he heard a voice say:

"I want a lift."

It was rather a rude voice, and when he looked he saw a boy as blackened and bent as a winter twig, and no sooner had Mr. Pengachoosa gotten down than the boy quickly scrambled into his seat.

As Mr. Pengachoosa set off up the hill he tried doing little dances with his toes, but the boy would not laugh, and the bicycle began to feel heavier.

He tried flapping his ears, but the boy would not laugh, and the bicycle felt heavier still.

He tried pretending to slip, but the boy did not laugh, and the bicycle felt so heavy that he could hardly push it up to the top.

And when he reached the top and turned around he saw, not a boy, but a great giant grinning nastily at him.

Poor Mr. Pengachoosa had not known that what he thought was a boy was really a giant in disguise, and before he could run away the giant had picked him up and carried him off to his cave. There the giant locked him up in a dungeon at the back.

After Mr. Pengachoosa had gotten over the worst of his fright, he began to look around and discovered he was not alone, for in the corner sat a boy who was all dressed in icy blue with a hood that looked like snow. This Mr. Pengachoosa rightly guessed was the second brother, so together they sat and tried to think of a way to escape.

After a while they heard the giant approaching, and as he put his head in the doorway Mr. Pengachoosa suddenly remembered his gifts. He pulled out his poppy and held it to the giant's nose, and no sooner had the giant taken one breath than he fell down fast asleep. Then Mr. Pengachoosa tiptoed up and slipped the nut into his open mouth and the giant swallowed it. Then Mr. Pengachoosa and the boy ran away out of the cave and back to the hill where they saw a sad sight, for the weight of the giant had been so great that the bicycle was all bent. So Mr. Pengachoosa took out the button and wished for a new bicycle, and there it was. . . .

"You've put that needle in with the pins," said my hamster suddenly.

"Was that the end?" I asked, taking it out again. "What happened when the giant woke up?"

"He did not remember," said Hammy. "Not anything. He even forgot that he had been wicked, and he did not feel hungry because of the magic nut, so he did not bother to eat much and so gradually he got smaller and smaller the less he ate, until he became quite ordinary and not a giant any more."

When my mother and sister came into the room I gave my mother the workbasket. Then I picked up the button and popped it in too.

"It's no good now; its wish has been used up," I said to my hamster who was washing his ears.

"What nonsense you do talk to that hamster," said my sister. "Anyone would think he could understand you."

❧ 5 ❧

The Wishes

One day when my hamster was telling me about his grand-father and how kind he was, I suddenly felt a little cross.

"Was he always nice?" I said. "Didn't he have any faults at all?"

Hammy stopped and looked surprised.

"Oh, yes, he had his faults. Once he had one quite bad one; he often longed to be more important. . . ."

30

You see he was one of those people whom everybody liked but was not somehow very special or grand, and this, when he was in the wrong sort of mood, used to make him cross.

It happened one day, as he was watering his garden, that a very rich and grand man rode by in his own coach. Mr. Pengachoosa looked down at his muddy boots and his gardening trousers and suddenly wished out loud that he was rich and important in his own coach too, and the next moment—he never understood how—there he was in a coach, wearing marvelous clothes and driving down the road. He felt very pleased and excited but found he could not smile, for his face had grown so important that it did not smile very well.

The coach took him to a great house where everyone seemed to know him, and called him "Sir." They seemed to think he was the most important person there. All day long he would walk around the gardens watching the gardeners working, or wandering in and out of the many rooms of his large house, until one day, he heard a great band approaching the house. First came drums and trumpets, then soldiers, and last of all, seated high above the rest, on a beautiful golden chair carried by sweating bearers, came a supremely grand looking man. All around a crowd seemed to have collected and everyone muttered:

"The King. . . . The King. . . ."

As the king passed they bowed their heads. Mr. Pengachoosa found that as the king approached he too bowed his
head, and when he looked up the king had passed and was
being carried slowly on down the street. And suddenly, to be
the grandest person of all became more important than ever,
and he stamped his foot and said:

"I wish I were more important than that king!"

No sooner had he said it than he found he was; in fact
he was an emperor.

Where there had been his rich house, there now stood a
palace, so beautiful in the bright sunlight that it hurt his
eyes to look at it, and while he stood, lots of servants came
running with sunshades and cushions, and they carefully
guided him up the marble steps, through many rooms where
everyone bowed, to the throneroom where he was placed
on the throne.

The most he ever saw of people was the tops of their
heads, because whenever he looked at them they bowed.
And he never saw their backs at all for they always went
out of the room backwards, bowing low all the time. Once
one of them bumped into the person behind him and looked
so surprised that the Emperor Pengachoosa almost laughed,
but found that he could not because his face was now much
too dignified.

Then one day his cook brought him some fruit. He was so used to having only the best that when he saw it was small and withered he demanded to know why.

"It's the sun, sire," said the cook. "It will not stop shining and everything is going bad or getting dried up."

"I will tell it to stop!" cried Emperor Pengachoosa, and he went to the window.

"I order you to stop shining," he shouted. But the sun went on shining.

"Why won't it stop when I tell it?" thought Emperor Pengachoosa crossly. "It can't be more important than me. Yet it must be, because it goes on shining."

He thought a bit, then:

"I wish I were the sun," he said softly.

And there he was in the sky, glowing and burning. At last he felt he was really the most important thing in the world or out of it, and he shone and shone.

But one day, as he shone on a garden he saw the flowers starting to droop. The more he shone, the more they wilted, until out of the house came a man with a watering can who began to water them, and then at last they began to revive. The sun tried to help him, but all he did was to make them droop again. This made him sad and he said:

"That man must be more important than me for he makes them better while I only make them worse. I wish I could revive the flowers instead of scorching them."

And suddenly, there he was, back in his garden in his old gardening trousers, with his watering can in his hand, watering the flowers, and all around his feet there was a large puddle.

"Poor old Mr. Pengachoosa, did he mind?" I asked. "I mean being back at the beginning again?"

"I don't think so," he said. "Anyway, he never bothered about being more important after that."

❧ 6 ❧

The Two Brothers

I used to ask Hammy quite often why it was that I could hear him so well but no one else could. I had held him near my sister's ear but she had said that I was just being silly.

"Why don't you talk to them, even a few words, just to show that I am not lying?"

"It's not that," said Hammy slowly. "Even if I did talk to them—even if I shouted—they would not hear. You see it all depends on what sort of person you are. You have to be a very still sort of person, who can put all your attention onto what is in front of you, or you can't possibly hope to hear what is going on. It's really rather a gift, and people who haven't got it always say there is no such thing. I suppose it makes them feel they are not missing anything then. Funnily enough my grandfather had the gift too. He was much better at it than you. . . ."

He could even hear trees: not of course when he was walking or doing anything; then they were just trees. But when he was fishing, say, and had been for hours sitting there, getting quieter and quieter, then he did begin to hear things.

There was a tree just by the bank where he always fished, that all day long used to whisper its one story again and again.

"Once," it said, "two brothers came to live in my shade. There was a big one called Will and a little one called Ned. I don't think they had a house to go to, for they were very raggedly dressed. They built a shelter under me, near the water, and there they lived.

"Every morning Will would go to the farms nearby to work. He helped with the animals, and then as the summer wore on he helped bring in the harvest, and as autumn drew in he picked the apples from the orchards. And every evening he would bring home some sort of food for their supper. While he was away Ned would fish and play. He climbed trees, and swam and walked and slept. And when it was time for Will to come home he lit the fire and roasted whatever fish he had caught and waited.

"All went well, until one evening Will was late. Poor Ned waited, but he had not caught any fish or eaten much all day, and he began to get very hungry and very bored. He called for Will but got no answer, and so, just as he was about to curl up to sleep beside the fire, he noticed the mushrooms growing beside the water, and decided to cook some of them for supper.

"I tried to tell him not to, but he was one that could not hear; I tried to tell him that they had suddenly appeared one wild midsummer night and there they had been ever since, neither getting bigger or smaller nor changing shape in any way, but just staying there as if waiting to be eaten.

"But little Ned cooked them and ate them as he was bored and hungry.

"And then he disappeared. He vanished as he stood there with the spoon full of mushrooms in his hand, and as he vanished the mushrooms reappeared on the bank just as they had always been.

"When it was nearly dark Will came home. He called for

Ned and looked everywhere but he could not find him. I tried to tell him, I called:

" 'Will, Will, stamp out the mushrooms.'

"I think he almost heard, but somehow he was calling and looking so much he never seemed to hear more than his own name, and I fancy he may have thought it was Ned calling. After a while he went away.

"He never did find Ned. He began to do quite well, and even bought his own farm, but every month or so he would come back and look and he always seemed to hear me call, 'Will, Will.' I think that was why he did not give up, but he never could hear the rest of the sentence."

Then the tree fell silent as the wind dropped and Mr. Pengachoosa went on with his fishing.

Some days later when Mr. Pengachoosa was again on the bank, a young man came, and when he saw Mr. Pengachoosa he looked surprised and nodded. Then he sat down with his back against the tree and shut his eyes. When the next breeze came it began to drift through the tree's branches, and it made a sad calling noise.

"Willlll . . . Willlll . . ." it moaned, and then Mr. Pengachoosa guessed who the young man was, for he sat up and began to look up and all around him.

"Getting a bit windy," remarked Mr. Pengachoosa, and began to pack up his things. Folding up his rod in sections, and gathering up his sandwich basket, he managed to trample on some of the mushrooms growing on the bank. As he turned around to see that nothing was forgotten he trampled on some more, and when finally he started off he stepped on the last two and walked away.

As he reached the top of the bank he again heard the cry, "Will, Will," but this time it was different.

"Why are you so late? I've been waiting so long."

"Ned! Where have you been?"

"I haven't been anywhere. You look different, Will, taller."

"Of course I'm taller. Don't look so puzzled Ned, I've a lot to tell you."

"Where are we going?"

"Not here any longer, I've something to show you," and as he led him away to his farm Mr. Pengachoosa could still hear the excited questions.

Ned is quite old now, but he never did remember what happened to him. . . .

"Hammy, you said I was a person who could hear things, but I've never heard trees talking."

"Well, I said he was much better at it than you. Or perhaps he was just a better storyteller."

The Turnip Doll

Now that spring was almost here and I was allowed out much
more, I did not spend so much time with my hamster, and
days would go by without his saying a word. But one night,
as I was cleaning his cage, my mother came in to kiss me
good night before she went out to the theater. She looked
very pretty in a green dress, and wore a silver necklace set
with stones of the same green.

After she had gone I looked at Hammy and saw he had

his dreamy storytelling expression, so I picked him up and held him in my cupped hands. . . .

Once, long ago, there was a little girl, rather like you, and one day as she was playing alone in a field she noticed, from among the tall grasses, a dirty face looking out at her.

At first she was very frightened, but as the face looked desperate and pleading, she went a little nearer, and found a soldier, not very old, lying in the grass. He looked so tired and worried that she asked him who he was and what he was doing, and he explained that he was escaping and must hide and lie low for a little while. So, just as you would be, she was thrilled and took him to the barn to sleep. She brought him food to eat, and as he seemed happier she left him for the night.

The next morning, taking some bread, she hurried to the barn directly after breakfast to see if he was still there. He was, and while he ate his bread she talked to him, though he did not say much.

After breakfast he went to the stack of turnips in the corner of the barn and began to pick them over till he found one that he fancied, but instead of eating it as the little girl had expected, he took out a knife and began to give it a nick here and there till it began to look very like a little face.

Then every day he worked a bit making a little doll. Its head was the turnip, carefully fastened onto a body of sacking stuffed with hay. He made arms of braided straw so that every finger stood out straight, and the skirt, that had been sacking to start with, he sewed so carefully and colorfully with the thread the child brought him, that soon it was covered with birds and flowers and trees and people. Often as he sewed he told her stories or sang her songs. On the fifth morning when she came to the barn with his breakfast she found that he had gone, but he had left behind the finished doll for her.

Somehow, like you, she had never liked dolls very much; their faces she found hard, with their eyes staring straight ahead with no expression, but she found the little turnip doll was different, when she held it close to her face the little turnip face was soft. In fact as the doll grew older her little face grew softer and more wrinkled, till all the wrinkles made her look gay, almost as if she were laughing. But as the little girl grew older she played with her less, though she still kept her.

Even when she grew up and got married, she still kept the little turnip doll, and when she had a daughter, who later became your grandmother, she gave it to her.

The turnip doll had never been very strong even when

44

it was first made, and by now it was very old and its little goblin face was only half the size that it had been.

So soon after she had been given it, the little girl came crying up with a dusty straw body in one hand and a withered turnip in the other. And that was the end of the turnip doll. . . .

"Is that the end?" I asked disappointed. "What's it got to do with Mr. Pengachoosa?"

"Nothing really, except that he told it to me, and it wasn't quite the end, even though it was the end of the turnip doll. For you see when the little girl and her mother gathered up the broken pieces, they found, tucked in the stuffing of the body, a necklace made of silver and set with dark green stones. It was very lovely, and the mother realized that long ago the soldier must have put it into the stuffing as a present to her, and when her daughter was old enough she gave it to her."

"That was my grandmother you said. I wonder where . . . oh Hammy! It can't be the one my mother was wearing, can it? No . . . It can't be, because she never said anything about a turnip doll."

"She never knew anything about the turnip doll. Her mother never told her. Though what is strange is that the necklace has the crest of your father's family on it, so though the soldier and the little girl never married or even met again, their grandchildren did."

That night as I lay in bed I wondered how I could tell my mother the story of the necklace, but, as I thought, I began gradually to see that I never could tell her, for when I remembered what had happened the previous day, I knew she would not believe me.

It was when I had taken Hammy out. He seemed huddled and cross, and when I put him down on the floor, he had scuttled quickly under the sofa, and climbed up into the springs inside, and though I called and called he had not come out. My sister, who was reading, looked up.

"You can't call a hamster; it's not like a dog!"

I tried to explain, but she just made a face, and my mother said:

"It's only that she's very imaginative."

"You mean that she's the world's worst liar!"

It took me ages to get Hammy out. I had to turn the sofa upside down. And when I finally put him back in his cage, he shuffled into his nest box without a word so I almost wondered if they were right.

✿ 8 ✿

The Hunt

Now that it was nearly summer, I had hardly any time to talk to my hamster, for a girl called Annabelle, who was about my own age, had moved next door. She had brothers, and we were helping them to turn the little stream into a harbor for boats.

Annabelle's brother said that if we dug hard enough we might even be able to make a swimming pool, or at least a duck pond, but at the moment we just sailed boats that we had made. Mine was called *The Unicorn* and theirs were *The Phoenix, The Basilisk,* and *The Griffon.*

I used to feed my hamster quickly before I ran down, but I did not often take him out, for now when I did he hardly ever wanted to talk, and when he did he always seemed a little cross. I wished sometimes that he was more like his grandfather.

But that last morning it rained. It came down steady and slow all through breakfast, and as I was still not allowed to get wet, I had to stay in.

When I opened the window I could hear Annabelle and her brothers shouting and laughing because the stream was so full, but I could not go. So I got my hamster out of his cage and played with him.

Though he did not talk at first, he seemed less cross than lately, even a little affectionate, and as we sat on the window seat, watching the dripping trees, he said, almost to himself:

"I did not hibernate this winter. We can, you know, and now it is nearly summer and I feel very tired."

Suddenly, looking at his cross little face, I felt very fond of him. I held him close to my face so I could feel his softness.

"I'm sorry I haven't taken you out lately, it's just that I have been having such fun."

"Never mind, we all have our own lives to lead, and it's far better to play out of doors if you can. . . ."

49

There used to be twin girls called Delia and Clarice who lived quite near Mr. Pengachoosa. They were about your age, and were always outdoors, for they lived on the edge of a wood and all their lives had run wild. Their father was a gardener and away a lot, and their mother was dead. Mr. Pengachoosa said he hardly ever saw them with shoes on, and always in the same old clothes, though Mr. Pengachoosa hardly ever saw them anyway. He just heard a giggle from behind or above him while walking in the wood, or felt a nut lightly hit him. Sometimes, when he heard a rustle, if he turned quickly enough, he might see a fleeting glimpse of a bare foot.

Once when he was in the wood he heard a rustle and turned quickly, thinking it was them, but it was a slim white horse standing against the dark trees. He almost thought he had imagined it, for it leaped away so quickly when it saw him.

That autumn he went to the wood a lot, as it was chestnut time, and as he shuffled through the leaves he found, stuck deep into the base of a tree, a short white pole. What was remarkable was the glow coming from it. Mr. Pengachoosa managed to pull the pointed end out, and he carefully carried it home and stood it up on his mantelpiece before he went to bed.

The next morning, when he came down, he found that the flowers in the wallpaper behind the pole seemed a little bumpy. By afternoon they stood out from the wall in perfect relief and felt quite real to touch.

So he realized the pole must be magic in some way, and next morning he went back into the wood to find out what it was, or where it had come from, or why it was stuck in the tree.

When he reached the wood, the first snow of winter had fallen, and in the dusting of white he saw the footprints of a horse and two children leading through the wood and he decided to follow them. The footprints led through the deepest part of the wood and then seemed to disappear at the base of a cliff. Mr. Pengachoosa was just going to return, when he heard soft singing and noticed that it was coming from a cave, overhung with branches, that he had not at first noticed. When he looked in, he saw the horse standing there quietly, with Delia lying along his back braiding his mane, and Clarice leaning against his side braiding his tail.

The horse must have sensed Mr. Pengachoosa, for he suddenly flung up his head and looked around, and Delia almost fell off.

Mr. Pengachoosa quickly left them and went home, but after that he sometimes saw them again, for he often went back to the woods to see if he could find another pole. He was moving the one he had slowly around the room so as to have the walls covered with real roses.

Once he saw them climbing into a tree off the back of the horse; another night he heard the thunder of hoofs and a laugh go by his window.

Christmas came, and the next day Mr. Pengachoosa was lying half asleep by the fire, roasting chestnuts, when he heard a great commotion going on outside his window, and going to it, he saw the hounds from the hunt sniffing around. Then one great brindled hound put her head back and began to bay, and ran hard in the direction of the wood. The others joined in; then the whole pack, in full cry, sped away to the woods, followed by the huntsmen, and lastly the village lads with sticks and dogs.

Mr. Pengachoosa scrambled quickly into his coat. First he ran to the cottage on the edge of the wood, but the children had already heard the hounds, and as he came up he saw them running hard for the wood and calling. Then he saw the white horse suddenly appear, almost invisible against the white snow. Delia scrambled onto its back, and with Clarice running alongside, they all three vanished into the wood.

Mr. Pengachoosa stood helpless as he heard the hounds from the other side of the wood put up a howl as they momentarily lost the trail. Then suddenly, while he thought of the horse, he realized why the hounds were so wild and

53

excited, and he turned and began to run, panting, as fast as his fat legs could carry him for home, gasping, "I've been a fool—a fool!"

He raced upstairs, grabbed the pole, and stumbled downstairs again. Back across the garden he went, his breath coming in clouds.

"At least I know where they might be," he thought as he headed for the cliff, and all the time the baying of the hounds rang in his ears.

As he neared the cliff he heard the new steady note as they found the trail again and began to come nearer.

Mr. Pengachoosa, gasping, reached the cave, and there the three were huddling.

"Please forgive me," he managed to whisper, "I never guessed." And he held the pole out toward the horse.

Slowly it came forward and lowered its head. Then Mr. Pengachoosa placed the broken end of the pole against the stub on its forehead and the two joined together.

Then the unicorn, no longer a horse, and no longer huddled, stepped proudly to the mouth of the cave as the brindled hound, followed by the others, broke cover, and raced toward them. As the first hound leaped, Mr. Pengachoosa closed his eyes. Then he heard a strange high yapping sound and opened them again. At the unicorn's feet was a brindled puppy, about three months old, gamboling and yapping.

54

As the second hound leaped with jaws slavering, the unicorn touched it gently with its horn, and it seemed to shrink before their eyes, until it sat, blinking and shivering, and only twelve weeks old.

One by one they attacked and were tapped by the horn, until when the huntsmen broke cover they found all around their feet puppies rolling and playing.

The Master of Hounds picked up the brindled puppy, and it wriggled and tried to lick his chin.

Outside, as if waking from a dream, I saw the sun was shining, and heard Annabelle calling for me. I realized she had been calling for quite a time. Hammy was saying:

"And that is why there is no hunt here now, for somehow they never recovered from the disgrace of returning home, with every huntsman's arms full of wriggling, yapping puppies!"

I put Hammy down.

"I can't wait, they're calling me." I remembered to call "Thank you," as I raced downstairs, but I don't know if he heard me.

That night, as I came upstairs after tea I had a worried feeling of something I had forgotten, and as I entered the room and felt for the light, I knew something was wrong.

There was the cage, the door open . . . empty!

I called and called but I knew as I did so it was no use, for I remembered the time in the sofa.

Now it is night and I am lying in bed, remembering, and the thing that seems to come back most is his saying, "Never mind, we all have our own lives to lead." Maybe, at last, he is leading his.